A Gift For:

_____

From:

_____

Published in 2011 by Hallmark Books,
a division of Hallmark Cards, Inc.,
Kansas City, MO 64141
Visit us on the Web at Hallmark.com.

Editor: Mary Gentry
Art Director: Kevin Swanson
Designer: Mary Eakin
Production Artist: Dan Horton
Character Development: Adan Chung

ISBN: 978-1-59530-343-1
BOK6183

Printed and bound in China
OCT10

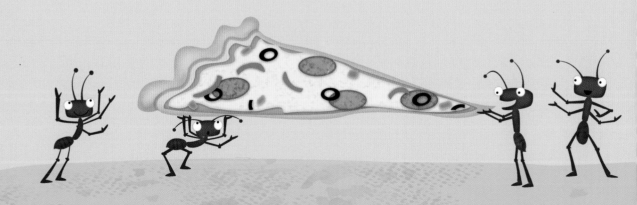

BUG 'em,
the Bighearted Bug
By Megan Haave

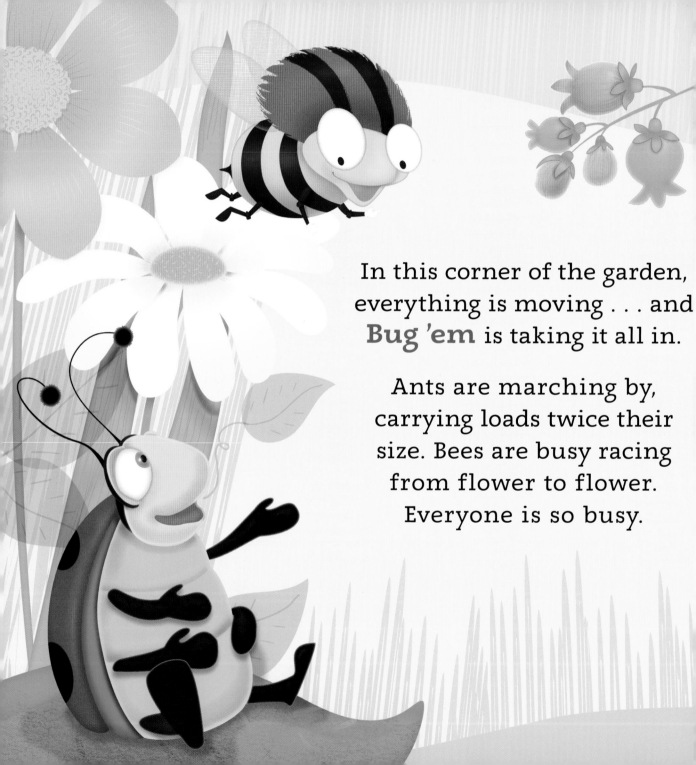

In this corner of the garden, everything is moving . . . and **Bug 'em** is taking it all in.

Ants are marching by, carrying loads twice their size. Bees are busy racing from flower to flower. Everyone is so busy.

Bug 'em is excited to jump in and help. If the ants need another back for carrying, why not his?

"Looks like quite the hefty job. What can I help you lug?" Bug 'em asks the ant in charge.

"How about moving that watermelon over here? It's for tomorrow's picnic," says the ant.

Bug 'em gathers all his oomph to roll the green giant. There's just one problem—it won't move one measly inch.

"Don't worry about it, Bug 'em. Leave it to us. We'll find a way."

Maybe Bug 'em would have better luck with the bees.

"Hi there. You sure look busy. Could you use some help? I may be new to this, but I'm willing to learn. Gimme a shot?"

"Think you can help us visit all these flowers?" asks the bee. "We've got lots of honey to make."

"I don't see why not," Bug 'em says with a little more confidence than he actually feels.

He gets off to a great start, racing from flower to flower, feeling speedier than he's ever felt.

But then the pollen starts to slow
him down. He'll never keep up with
the bees at this rate.

"Thanks for trying, but it might be faster if we just do it ourselves, Bug 'em."

"Hmm. I wonder what Fuzz the caterpillar is up to. Maybe he could use a hand," says Bug 'em.

"Whatcha doin, Fuzz?" asks Bug 'em. "Isn't it a little warm for a coat?"

"It's not a coat, Bug 'em. I'm trying to make a cocoon, but I don't think I'm doing it right. These things should come with a how-to book."

"Wish I could help. You're doing a great job, though. That's the coolest cocoon I've ever seen."

"I'm not so sure. We'll see."

Bug 'em goes to bed that night wishing he could have helped his friends. If only he were stronger or faster or better at making cocoons—then maybe he'd be able to help.

Bug 'em wakes up the next morning
and thinks he might be dreaming.

"Hey, Bug 'em! Wake up! You were right!" yells Fuzz.

"I didn't think my cocoon would turn out, but you said I could do it. Thanks, Bug 'em. You really helped!"

"I helped?!" Bug 'em beams.

That gives him an idea. He runs to the anthill.

As the ants get ready to leave for their picnic, they notice someone has left them a message.

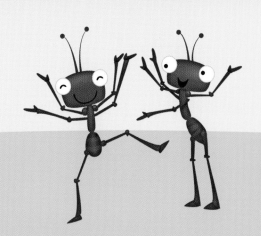

"Are we ready for this picnic
or what? **1-2-3, lift!**"

While the ants carry off their feast,
Bug 'em is headed to the bees' hive.

When the bees are flying home, they see something on the branch above their hive . . .

WORLD'S SPEEDIEST BEES

The bees buzz with pride and fly home as fast as they've ever gone.

"Sweet!"

"We'll make the world's best honey, too!"

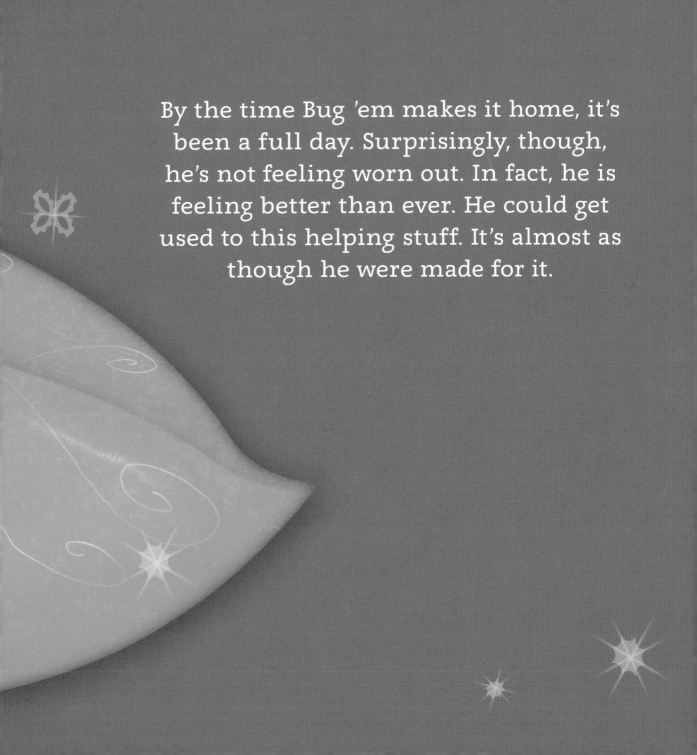

By the time Bug 'em makes it home, it's been a full day. Surprisingly, though, he's not feeling worn out. In fact, he is feeling better than ever. He could get used to this helping stuff. It's almost as though he were made for it.

If you have enjoyed this book
or it has touched your life in some way,
we would love to hear from you.

Please send your comments to:
Hallmark Book Feedback
P.O. Box 419034
Mail Drop 215
Kansas City, MO 64141

Or e-mail us at:
booknotes@hallmark.com